DESTI N ATION
VERACRUZ

by Herón Márquez

Lerner Pu   inneapolis

PHOTO ACKNOWLEDGMENTS

Cover photo © Charlene E. Friesen/DDB Stock Photo. All inside photos courtesy of: Adalberto Rios Szalay/Visor, pp. 5, 6, 9, 14, 15, 16, 17, 20, 24, 27, 38, 39, 42, 48, 52, 54, 56, 57 (both), 62, 63, 65, 66-67, 68; © D. Donne Bryant/DDB Stock Photo, pp. 10, 13, 31, 41, 53, 64; © Kevin G. Hall, pp. 11, 45, 47; © John Curtis/DDB Stock Photo, p. 18; Port of Veracruz, pp. 19, 44; © Charlene E. Friesen/DDB Stock Photo, p. 22; Keith Hay/American Petroleum Institute, p. 23; © Suzanne Murphy-Larronde, p. 26 (top); Trustees of the British Museum, p. 26 (bottom); Sexto Sol/Visor, pp. 32, 61; Reuters/Corbis-Bettmann, p. 29; Bettmann, p. 30; Archive Photos, pp. 33, 34, 36; UPI/Corbis-Bettmann, p. 35; AP/Wide World Photos, p. 40; © Chris R. Sharp/DDB Stock Photo, p. 46.

I wish to dedicate this book to my wife, Traecy, who showed remarkable patience during this whole thing.

Website address: www.lernerbooks.com

LIBRARY OF CONGRESS CATALOGING-IN-PUBLICATION DATA

Márquez, Herón
    Destination Veracruz / by Herón Márquez.
       p. cm. – (Port cities of North America)
    Includes index.
    Summary: An introduction to the port city of Veracruz, describing its geography, history, economy, and daily life.
    ISBN 0-8225-2791-X (lib. bdg. : alk. paper)
    1. Veracruz (Veracruz, Mexico) — Juvenile literature.
[1. Veracruz (Veracruz, Mexico)] I. Title. II. Series.
F1391.V4M37 1998
972'.62 — DC21   97-16616

Manufactured in the United States of America
1 2 3 4 5 6 – JR – 03 02 01 00 99 98

Our thanks to Mr. Kevin Hall of the Journal of Commerce and Commercial *for his help in preparing this book.*

The glossary that begins on page 68 gives definitions of words shown in **bold type** in the text.

CONTENTS

CHAPTER ONE

LAY OF THE LAND

A pair of cranes load a ship at the Port of Veracruz, the busiest seaport in Mexico.

Without the Port of Veracruz, there would be no city of Veracruz. The city, founded by Spaniards in 1519, has grown and prospered along with the port and its trade capabilities. Veracruz's expansion has helped make Mexico into one of the world's leading trading nations. Each day Mexican oil, coffee, and cars sail across the Gulf of Mexico to the United States and Canada in North America, across the Atlantic Ocean to Europe, or around the Yucatán Peninsula to South America. In exchange for these goods, Mexico receives everything from cold hard cash to computer software. This worldwide exchange enables people in Mexico and elsewhere to drive U.S. automobiles, to drink Colombian coffee, and to watch Japanese televisions.

The Port of Veracruz, Mexico, is a natural harbor on the Bay of Campeche. This bay is part of the Gulf of Mexico—an arm of the Atlantic Ocean. The port is part of the eastern coastal state of Veracruz, Mexico. On a map the long, narrow state of Veracruz looks a lot like a caterpillar, curling for about 500 miles along the shores of the Gulf of Mexico. From this excellent location, the Port of Veracruz is the hub of a large web of trade stretching across the world. For example, just southeast of Veracruz are the Caribbean nations of Cuba, Jamaica, Haiti, and the Dominican Republic. Farther east are the open waters of the Atlantic Ocean, by which ships can reach the markets of South America, Africa, Europe, Canada, and the eastern United States. From the Port of Veracruz it is only a short trip south to the Panama Canal, which provides easy access to the Pacific Ocean and the markets of Southeast Asia and China. And finally highways and railroads link the port to U.S. and Mexican cities.

The port is in the tropics—a hot and humid region near the equator. The Port of Veracruz's average daily temperature is about 78 degrees but can climb above 100 degrees in the summer. The port, the first built in the Americas, lies along a very swampy stretch of coast, parts of which have been filled in to provide solid land for the port facilities.

> ➤ The state of Veracruz is swampy because rainfall and melting snow flow to the coast from the Eastern Sierra Madre, a mountain range that runs through the state.
>
> ➤ Almost 35 percent of Mexico's water supply is in the state of Veracruz.

For many centuries, Veracruz was known as the City of the Dead because the climate killed so many people. The hot swamplands that once covered the area were a breeding ground for mosquitoes, which spread deadly malaria to

◀ **The City of the Dead**

Swamps like this one cover much of the lowlands in the state of Veracruz, which lies on the east coast of Mexico.

humans. The humidity and heat of Veracruz are still uncomfortable, especially during the summer months. But the rest of the territory has changed a lot as the city of Veracruz has grown up around the port. The port and its piers, warehouses, roads, buildings, and other facilities sprawl across several miles of the downtown area. The port covers approximately 1,410 acres, 495 of which are water in the harbor. Veracruz has close to 20 piers with water depths ranging from 30 to 40 feet. The other 915 acres of dry land hold 22 warehouses as well as sheds, open storage yards, workshops, grain silos, and other facilities to aid in the shipping and receiving of goods.

While Veracruz began life as a Spanish military port, only one pier is still designated for military traffic—the Navy Pier in the southeastern corner of the harbor. The port is primarily an extremely busy commercial harbor.

Almost 25 percent of all annual exports and imports shipped by sea to and from Mexico passes through Veracruz. Veracruz handles more **containerized** cargo than any other port in Mexico. More than 15 companies at the port ship and receive containerized cargo headed to and from the United States, northern Europe, South America, Mediterranean countries, and islands in the Caribbean Sea. Dockside cranes lift the heavy containers on and off vessels. Sometimes ships are equipped with roll-on/roll-off (ro-ro) ramps, which allow trucks to drive directly onboard to deliver or pick up cargoes.

A partially loaded container ship rests beside the wharf, awaiting the rest of its cargo.

A Tour of the Port ▶ Three **breakwaters**—the North, the Northeast, and the Southeast—shield the Port of Veracruz from the rougher ocean waters. Although weather conditions are generally favorable, seasonal hurricanes pass through the area each year from June through September. The rest of the time, gentler **trade winds** blow from the north and the east.

The port entrance is also protected by rocky shelves and is surrounded by islands, reefs, and shallow water. As a result of the tricky entrance, pilots from the Veracruzan division of the National Syndicate of Port Pilots must steer ships in and out of the harbor. The pilots usually board vessels outside the breakwaters but will meet them beyond the reefs if necessary. Once inside the harbor, tugboats—small, maneuverable vessels with powerful engines—help guide ships to their docks. Two tugs are required for the largest freighters.

A tugboat, helping a larger vessel to navigate the harbor, pushes in the right direction.

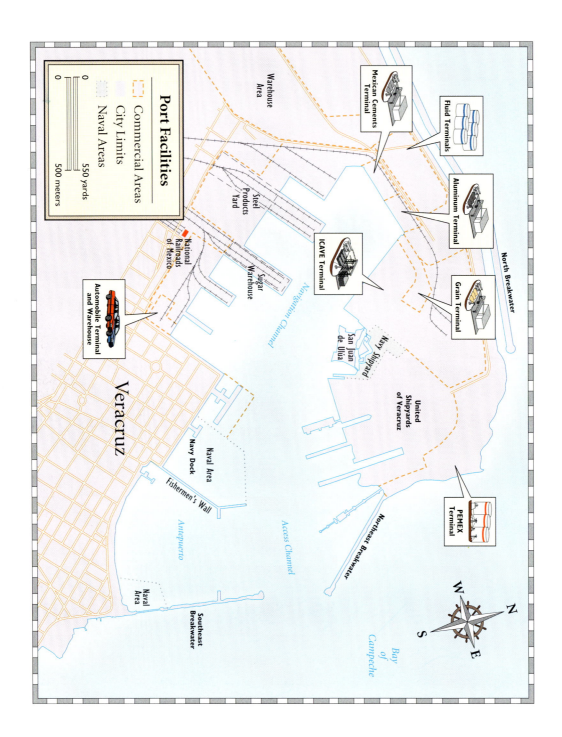

Port Facilities

Commercial Areas
City Limits
Naval Areas

0
0
0
550 yards
500 meters

Warehouse Area

Mexican Cements Terminal

Fluid Terminals

Aluminum Terminal

Grain Terminal

North Breakwater

Steel Products Yard

ICAVE Terminal

National Railroads of Mexico

Sugar Warehouse

Navigation Channel

Automobile Terminal and Warehouse

San Juan de Ulúa

Navy Shipyard

United Shipyards of Veracruz

PEMEX Terminal

Veracruz

Navy Dock

Naval Area

Fishermen's Wall

Northeast Breakwater

Antepuerto

Access Channel

Naval Area

Southeast Breakwater

Bay of Campeche

N
W   E
S

12

The Fishermen's Wall, a breakwater within the harbor, juts out toward the port's shipyard.

The Access Channel, which is about 40 feet deep, passes between the Northeast and the Southeast Breakwaters. To the south of the port entrance is the Antepuerto, a harbor used by private boaters to dock their pleasure craft. Two more breakwaters—the Fishermen's Wall and a smaller deflective wall—separate the Antepuerto from the rest of the port. A portion of the Antepuerto is set aside for tourist development, and the southernmost corner is reserved for use by the navy. The Navy Pier itself lies to the northwest, on the other side of the Fishermen's Wall.

Across from the Antepuerto and north of the harbor entrance is Mexican Petroleum (PEMEX), the national oil company. The PEMEX Wharf, about 1,020 feet long with a water depth of about 30 feet, has a pipeline that can load and unload 5,000 barrels of fuel oil, gasoline, or diesel fuel per hour. The warehouses at the PEMEX terminal can store 215,000 barrels of fuels. About 600,000 tons of oil pass through Veracruz each year, making it a major oil port.

➤ Run by Mexico's government, PEMEX is the only oil company in the country.

➤ Although the company has a terminal at the Port of Veracruz, PEMEX operates independently of the port. For example, oil cargoes are not counted in with the port's yearly tonnage statistics.

➤ A barrel of petroleum equals about 42 gallons.

Two ships sit beside the PEMEX Wharf, which is run by the national oil company. The yellow floats around the larger vessel will prevent any spilled oil from escaping into the harbor's waters.

Two gantry cranes unload a container ship while trucks wait nearby to carry the cargo from the port to customers in central Mexico.

> Container traffic is measured in 20-foot equivalent units (TEUs). One TEU represents a container that is 20 feet long, 8 feet wide, and 8.5 or 9.5 feet high.

To the west of the PEMEX terminal is the port's large shipyard, operated by United Shipyards of Veracruz, a company that builds and repairs commercial cargo ships. The shipyard covers an area of about 89 acres, including two **dry docks** and three floating docks. Roads and railways connect the shipyard to the rest of the port and beyond. At the southwestern corner of the United Shipyards facility is the navy's shipyard, which has one dry dock.

The container terminal of the International Container Associates of Veracruz (ICAVE) handles containerized cargo and lies next to the two shipyards. Yards for storing and repairing containers curve northward behind the shipyard. From these yards, the 85-acre terminal area stretches out to meet the water. Four **gantry cranes** and five smaller cranes at the ICAVE Container Terminal's wharf load and unload the containers directly from ships. Forklifts take the containers to the storage yards, where the boxes are stacked on top of one another to save space. The container facility can move 52 boxes per hour, but ICAVE intends eventually to build another wharf to increase the efficiency of the operation.

The Access Channel turns sharply to the northwest and becomes the Navigation Channel just past the shipyard and the container terminal. On the northern side of the bend is the port's most imposing feature, the island of San Juan de Ulúa, which provides a natural breakwater next to the canal. Over the years, the port has expanded around the island, which is connected to the mainland by a short road going over a bridge. Formerly the site of a fortress and a government headquarters, the island houses a museum these days.

In 1535 Spanish officials began building San Juan de Ulúa, once the port's main headquarters.

Past San Juan de Ulúa, at the northwestern-most end of the Navigation Channel, four specialty terminals handle the shipping and receiving of **bulk cargoes** of aluminum, fluids, grains, and cement. The Aluminum Terminal can move 110 tons of materials per hour and handles aluminum ingots (bars) and bulk mineral cargo. Ships at the Aluminum Terminal, primarily an import facility, can unload their cargoes directly onto trucks or trains. The terminal also has warehouses that can store 6,900 tons of bulk materials. Trains bring loads of cement to the Mexican Cements Terminal, which can transfer 110 tons per hour, for export to other countries. Corn, wheat, sunflower seeds, and other agricultural bulk items pass through the Grain Terminal. The Grain Terminal's warehouses can hold 50,000 tons and can handle more than 275 tons per hour of operation. Incoming ships can offload their cargoes directly into trucks. Large silos near the dock

Dockworkers fill a truck directly from a ship at the Grain Terminal.

can also store the grains, which are later loaded into railcars for the trip to Mexico City (the nation's capital) and other inland destinations. The Fluid Terminals, located behind the other three specialty facilities, handle liquid bulk cargo such as vegetable oil and molasses.

To the west of the waterfront at the northwestern end of the port are large warehouse yards and an area reserved for port development. Customs offices, where foreign merchants must check in their goods before entering Mexico, are located behind the warehouses. The Integral Port Administration of Veracruz (APIVER), an independent government agency that runs the port, has its offices here as well. The Port of Veracruz's trucking headquarters, including a large parking lot for trailers, lies in the port's westernmost corner.

Behind the port's warehouses, laborers decide which cargoes to place onto which trucks for delivery to industrial cities in Veracruz and in other Mexican states.

Workers drive new automobiles into the hold of a car-carrier ship.

At the northwesternmost end of the Navigation Channel, the waterfront curves back to the southeast, where wharves and warehouses belonging to the city of Veracruz line the shore. Most of the facilities on the western side of the Navigation Channel are multipurpose or general cargo terminals, but among them are specialty areas, including a steel products yard and the port's sugar warehouse. Port officials plan to build a refrigerated warehouse here.

At the Navigation Channel's southeasternmost end, where it joins the Access Channel, is the Automobile Terminal. The terminal's warehouse can store 2,130 cars and can transfer 120 cars per hour of operation. When loading a car-carrier ship, automobiles drive up a special ramp at the dock, over the ship's connecting ro-ro ramp, and into the vessel's cargo hold.

The automobile warehouse has road and rail connections so that trucks and trains can bring the cars to the wharf for shipment. Railroad tracks extend onto almost all the piers to ease loading and unloading cargo. The tracks lead to the nearby terminal of National Railroads of Mexico, the state-owned railroad company. From there passengers and cargo can travel all over the country. A national four-lane highway links Mexico City to Veracruz. On this highway, travel between the two cities takes less than five hours. The road helps Veracruz's goods to reach a market of 40 million people in the capital and neighboring states. An international airport less than 10 miles away connects Veracruz to points all over the globe.

The state of Veracruz has 1,777 miles of four-lane highways. The roads allow the port's goods to reach 40 million customers in Mexico, including the country's heavily populated capital.

20

The Cost of Progress ➤ The city and port of Veracruz have grown significantly since their founding hundreds of years ago, but the advances and progress have not come without costs. The port has turned Veracruz into a leading industrial center, complete with the air, water, and land pollution that go hand in hand with unregulated industrialization. The problems have been worsened by two factors: the lack of tight environmental regulations in Mexico and the presence of vast oil reserves in the Gulf of Mexico. A poor nation, Mexico needs money to modernize, so developing the oil industry has been a high priority. The government built oil facilities in Veracruz and also established several new ports to ship the millions of gallons of oil all over the world. The sights—and smells—of oil facilities in and around the Port of Veracruz are a reminder not only of the natural wealth of the country but also of the costs of cashing in on that wealth without thinking about the environment.

A Shining Future ➤ The cash-strapped Mexican government has decided to get out of running the port, which APIVER has administered since 1994. Although the government still owns many parts of the port, it has invited private companies to take over operation of most terminals and to invest their own money to improve services and facilities. In 1995, for example, ICAVE paid the Mexican government for the right to operate the container terminal at the port. ICAVE—a partnership between a Filipino company and a Mexican company—has decided to invest more money to upgrade the container operations.

> ➤ ICAVE increased efficiency at the container terminal by 50 percent within one year of taking over operations, in part by computerizing the terminal's services.

Port administrators and the Mexican government have determined that they also need to spend money to improve the aging port. In the mid-1990s, the government estimated that it would spend about $200 million dollars by the year 2000 for harbor improvements. In 1996 workers dredged the harbor to 40 feet. Other plans call for a new cargo terminal wharf at the western end of the port, a cruise ship terminal, refrigerated warehouses, eating and laundry facilities, and a money exchange house. Officials have also committed to remodeling old, outdated wharves and terminals.

Port administrators expect that the improvements will more than triple the amount of cargo handled at Veracruz. Officials believe that this increase will create thousands of new jobs, giving the city a helpful boost into the twenty-first century and securing the port's place as Mexico's gateway to the world.

Vessels that come in and out of Veracruz can receive repairs at the port's commercial shipyard. Updating equipment and offering better shipping services will continue to attract business to the port.

OIL AND WATER DON'T MIX

Oil. Three tiny letters containing so much power. Cars can't run without it. Wars have been fought over it. Oil has driven the tremendous economic progress of many countries, including Mexico. The Gulf of Mexico and the Bay of Campeche are especially rich in oil. In fact there are more than 2,600 oil wells in the state of Veracruz. The presence of so much oil, however, has not come without environmental costs such as air, land, and water pollution.

The oil refineries and petrochemical complexes near the Port of Veracruz are a large part of why the harbor waters are so dirty. Occasionally a spill at a refinery will produce an oil slick. Burning and processing at the plants result in smoggy air and sulfur emissions that damage crops. Sometimes the plants illegally dump their wastes on the ground or in the water. And because few laws regulate the refineries' operation, they can run inefficiently and produce dangerous amounts of by-products.

PEMEX, the government-run oil company, has not always listened to residents' concerns about oil in the waterways and sulfur-damaged crops. As a result, citizens have filed many lawsuits to get the company to change its practices. In the 1990s, the government finally responded with environmental initiatives, such as a 1991 law that limited waste dumping, as well as better enforcement of existing laws.

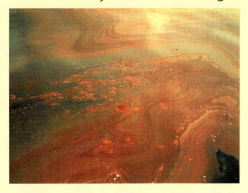

CHAPTER TWO

THE RICH TOWN OF THE TRUE CROSS

Mexico's Earliest Culture ▶ Beginning about 3,200 years ago, a group called the Olmecs made their home near modern-day Veracruz. Many scientists consider the Olmecs the original culture of Mexico. The Olmecs were skilled artists and builders. They brought blocks of stone hundreds of miles from the Eastern Sierra Madre to the Gulf Coast, where they erected massive buildings and carved large stone heads—many weighing 20 tons or more. The Olmecs were farmers as well. Their fertile croplands allowed them to grow extra food, which they traded with other peoples in the interior of Mexico. Some scientists believe that the

Small villages like this one have dotted Mexico's Gulf Coast for centuries.

25

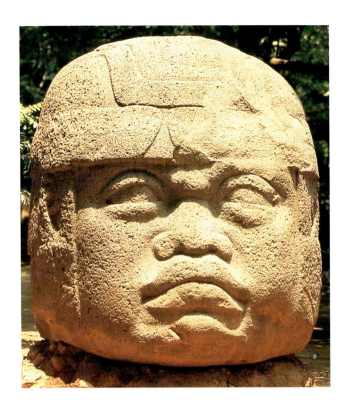

Olmec craftspeople created finely detailed works from jade (below), but these early inhabitants of Mexico are better known for their giant basalt head sculptures (left).

Olmecs spread their influence through trade rather than through conquest. The Olmec trade networks stretched south to the Yucatán Peninsula, where the Mayan culture flourished. The Olmecs also traded with groups in the central part of Mexico, including the Zapotec people from around Teotihuacán, a large religious and market center near present-day Mexico City.

The Olmecs exchanged fish, fruits, and works of art for stone and jade, which they considered more precious than gold. Olmec artisans made delicate jade artwork, such as figurines (small statues). The finished objects were then traded for raw materials such as obsidian, a stone used to make tools.

A Shift of Power ➤ About 2,100 years ago, when the Olmec culture began to decline, the Zapotecs in central Mexico grew more powerful. The rise of the Zapotecs shifted the focus of Mexican civilization from the Veracruz area to the highlands around Teotihuacán. The shift in power came in part because the city was next to a large deposit of obsidian. The obsidian helped make Teotihuacán the most important marketplace in Mexico, especially for Gulf Coast residents, who needed an outlet for their trade goods. Archaeological finds along the coast indicate that several small towns near present-day Veracruz served as commercial centers for the exchange of goods from central Mexico.

Centuries ago only sandy beaches (above) existed where the Port of Veracruz's docks would one day bustle with traffic.

Eventually people began migrating from Teotihuacán to the Veracruz area. After living near Veracruz for some time, these nomads returned to central Mexico and helped to found the Toltec culture. The Toltecs were mighty warriors who lived in and ruled most of central Mexico from A.D. 950 to A.D. 1200. Master craftspeople as well, the Toltecs built one of the nation's most impressive cities, Tula, in the modern-day Mexican state of Hidalgo. Because of their historical links to the Gulf Coast, the Toltecs eventually became the Veracruz region's major trading partners.

In about A.D. 1300, the Aztecs rose to power in Tenochtitlán (present-day Mexico City) and replaced the Toltecs. From central Mexico, the Aztec empire stretched hundreds of miles east to Veracruz and to other parts of the Gulf Coast. The Aztecs built a complex, hierarchical society with the emperor, regarded as a god, at the highest rank. Priests and nobles came next, and at the lowest rank were the common people. Through a vast system of taxation backed with military might, the Aztecs forced nearly every community between central Mexico and Central America to pay tribute. In exchange for military protection, the various nations paid the Aztecs tribute in the form of food, cotton clothing, feathers, precious stones, and other valuables.

➤ In 1994 archaeologists uncovered an ancient city near the coastal village of El Pital, about 60 miles north of the Port of Veracruz. The site contained figurines and ceramic items from Teotihuacán, as well as many farm fields. These findings indicate that El Pital had strong trading ties with Teotihuacán and might also have been an important food-producing region.

◀ A Good Day to Land

Meanwhile, across the Atlantic Ocean in Europe, Spain was looking for new sources of wealth to help build a sizable empire. When the Spaniards arrived in April 1519, about 10 million people lived in Mexico.

Wearing ceremonial clothes for a special occasion, these three men are descendants of the Aztecs who controlled Mexico in the early 1500s.

Led by Hernán Cortés, the Spanish forces landed just a few miles north of what would become the Port of Veracruz. On July 10, 1519, in this hot, humid, mosquito-ridden, inhospitable swamp, Cortés founded the first Spanish settlement in Mexico. He called it La Villa Rica de la Vera Cruz (the Rich Town of the True Cross), but the name was later shortened to Veracruz. From this colony, the Spanish set about conquering Mexico. The Spaniards indirectly benefited from the harsh requirements that the Aztecs had long been imposing on their subjects. Gulf Coast native peoples were restless and resentful toward the rulers. As a result, they willingly joined Spanish efforts to

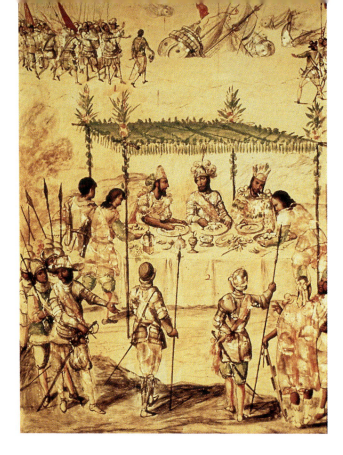

This painting portrays two scenes from the Spanish conquest of Mexico. In the first, the explorer Hernán Cortés destroys his ships so that his crew cannot abandon him at their inhospitable landing spot. In the second scene, the Spaniards eat a meal with Aztec officials.

overthrow the Aztec empire. After two years of fighting, Cortés and his allies took over Mexico. The Spaniards then focused on building up the Port of Veracruz.

To escape the unfavorable conditions of the swampy beach, the Spanish settlers moved their town several times. The original site became known as La Antigua, or the Old Town. When the settlement moved to its final location near the island of San Juan de Ulúa in 1599, the town retained the name of Veracruz. In 1601 workers built the first pier, along with large wooden warehouses. A town made of wooden planks soon sprang up around the new facilities.

After the Mexican conquest, the Spaniards forced the Gulf Coast natives, their one-time allies, to work the fields and to expand the port. Many natives died because of harsh working conditions or from European diseases against which the native people had no natural defenses. Many of the Spaniards themselves died of malaria or were killed by natives. In need of a continuous source of cheap labor, Spain began forcibly importing Africans to the Spanish colonies in the Americas. Spain brought an estimated total of 600,000 slaves from Africa to Mexico via the Port of Veracruz.

HERO OR HEEL?

In all of history, there have been few people as brave, foolhardy, or lucky as the controversial Hernán Cortés. The Spanish explorer is credited with founding the Port of Veracruz, thus reshaping the area's history forever. Europeans considered him the hero of the Mexican conquest. But in Mexico, Cortés is more often seen as a villain and not a champion. Although Cortés launched a new country and created a thriving port, he was also a brutal warlord, responsible for helping to destroy Mexico's native cutures.

Spanish leaders had designated Veracruz as the only port through which Mexican gold and silver could be shipped to Spain. The amount of wealth stored at the port made it a tempting target for attacks by English and French pirates. The raids forced Spain to set up a fort on San Juan de Ulúa Island to protect the settlement and the harbor. In 1609 construction began on Veracruz's municipal palace. Crews constructed storage facilities in front of the palace to house the gold and silver destined for export to Spain. By 1700 a stone wall with seven bastions encircled the city. While the wall kept out marauders, it also trapped citizens inside for long periods of time. As a result, the city's growth was slow, and poor sanitation caused many health problems. By the time the walls were torn down to allow the city and port to expand, the wealth leaving Mexico through Veracruz had transformed Spain into a major European power.

A drawing made during Veracruz's early years as a Spanish colony shows the city and the port.

War and Politics ➤ Veracruz became a vital commercial, social, and political link to Spain, second only to Mexico City in importance. Nearly all trade between Spain and Mexico passed through the port, and Veracruz's influence increased as Mexico's economy and society grew. By the 1800s, Mexicans were seeking to free themselves from Spain. They succeeded in 1821 after a lengthy revolutionary struggle. In 1822 Agustín de Iturbide, a Spanish official who had joined the Mexican rebel forces, declared himself the first emperor of Mexico. But his reign lasted only a few months. Wanting a more democratic form of government, General Antonio López de Santa Anna of Veracruz overthrew Iturbide and proclaimed the first Republic of Mexico. By 1824 legislators in Veracruz adopted a federal constitution, and General Guadalupe Victoria, also from Veracruz, became the first president of Mexico.

Throughout the 1800s, as in previous centuries, the importance and strategic location of Veracruz made it a target for foreign attack. During the mid-1800s, troops from France and the United States occupied Veracruz on several occasions.

Born in Veracruz state, General Antonio López de Santa Anna began his military career as a soldier in Spain's colonial army, which was fighting against Mexican rebels. He deserted the army with Agustín de Iturbide and helped to win Mexico's independence from Spain.

The fighting and foreign occupations made entering or leaving the port too dangerous for private ships. For this reason, Veracruz developed at a slow pace. Only when peace was restored in the late 1800s could Mexico devote its energy to upgrading the Port of Veracruz. In 1873 President Sebastián Lerdo de Tejada inaugurated the Veracruz–Mexico City railroad line, providing a direct link from the port to Mexico's markets. Workers added a major pier to the port in 1880.

Crews lay railroad track at the port around 1890.

In 1877 an army general named Porfirio Díaz seized the presidency and began modernizing Mexico. He brought in foreign companies to update the nation's roads, railways, and ports. The city of Veracruz received telephone service in 1892, and the port gained a wharf in 1895.

Rebel troops occupy a train in Veracruz in 1914 during the revolt against President Porfirio Díaz.

Builders used state-of-the-art engineering technology to fill shallow ocean waters near the port with earth. This process, called reclamation, expanded the port's facilities by dozens of acres. A paved road connected San Juan de Ulúa Island to the mainland, linking the port directly to the city.

While Díaz had done much to bring the country into the twentieth century, he had been cruel in his methods. Wanting a fairer government and a more equal distribution of land, the Mexican people revolted. Díaz fled to Europe, sailing from Veracruz in 1911. The revolution that followed Díaz's departure again made the port and city of Veracruz unstable and vulnerable to foreign intervention. To influence the course of the war, the United States invaded Veracruz in 1914 to choke off arms shipments to the Mexican government's forces.

The U.S. plan was successful, and rebel commander Venustiano Carranza became president. Dissatisfied with this outcome, other rebel leaders extended the fighting. Veracruz served as the site of President Carranza's provisional government for several months during the struggle. The revolution ended in 1920, and the political situation in Mexico stabilized. These events greatly benefited Veracruz and its economy. Three new piers were built in 1920, followed by two more in 1936. Explorers found oil deposits in the Gulf of Mexico along the Veracruz coast, and U.S. and European oil firms began developing the sites. Mexican officials became unhappy with the foreign control of Mexican oil. President Lázaro Cárdenas nationalized the sites (put them under state ownership).

➤ In 1938 the Mexican government took over foreign-owned oil companies and created PEMEX. Mexican oil workers striking in Poza Rica, Veracruz, prompted the government's move.

The hunger for oil and petroleum products increased during and after World War II (1939–1945). Oil prices rose steadily, and Mexico used its petroleum earnings to develop the Port of Veracruz. By 1956 port officials had added six more piers. During the 1950s and 1960s, the Mexican government also encouraged **import substitution** policies. That is, instead of buying goods from other countries, the government helped local industries to grow and prosper so that Mexicans could make their own products. Authorities set up regional centers for textile, iron, and steel production in places such as Mexico City, Monterrey, Guadalajara, and Veracruz. The policies helped Veracruz become a national leader in the production and exportation of steel, aluminum, and machine tools and turned Veracruz into the largest industrialized port in Mexico.

Energy Crisis ➤ In 1972 the Organization of Petroleum Exporting Countries (OPEC), a **cartel** of nations that still controls most of the world's oil, refused to sell petroleum to countries that opposed certain OPEC policies. OPEC's decision threw the United States and many European countries into an energy crisis. Oil prices skyrocketed. Eager to cash in, Mexico increased its efforts at petroleum exploration. By 1981 the country had 90 billion barrels of proven oil reserves, and scientists believed there might be as much as 160 billion barrels more. These discoveries along the Gulf Coast made Mexico the nation with the fifth-largest oil reserves in the world.

The energy crisis turned out to be a double-edged sword for Mexico. High oil prices

Offshore oil rigs (left), *able to drill in deep ocean water, played an important part in Mexico's post–World War II prosperity.*

PEMEX's headquarters are in a tall, white building overlooking the port.

brought in billions of dollars for the country, which grew accustomed to a large income. Mexico began taking out larger and larger loans for development, certain of its ability to repay. But with all the increased production, oil supplies soon rose high above demand for the product. As a result, world oil prices dropped suddenly in 1981, and Mexico was left high and dry. With less oil money to spend, improvements on ports and other facilities stopped while the nation concentrated on paying its debts.

➤ Port planners completed a special pier and storage facilities for PEMEX in 1975.

Drawing a Crowd ▶ During the late 1980s, Veracruz State and the Port of Veracruz began looking for new sources of money. City and port officials, focusing on the area's famous Spanish architecture, spicy cuisine, and lively music, sought to increase Veracruz's share of the Mexican tourism industry. By the 1990s, the strategy was paying off, and hundreds of thousands of people flocked to Veracruz each year, most of them from Mexico City and other places within the country.

Mexican tourists swim and lounge on the deck of a hotel pool at Veracruz.

In 1994 Mexico joined Canada and the United States in the North American Free Trade Agreement (NAFTA), a pact that is removing trade barriers among the three nations. Of the three nations, Mexico has benefited most from NAFTA, in part because it is less developed than its two partners. Wages are lower and government regulation of business is weaker in Mexico than in the United States or Canada. Foreign companies can make products cheaply in Mexico and send them elsewhere in North America, taking full advantage of NAFTA.

Mexican president Carlos Salinas de Gortari (back left), U.S. president George Bush, and Canadian prime minister Brian Mulroney watch as trade officials Jaime Serra Puche, Carla Hills, and Michael Wilson sign NAFTA in 1992. The treaty went into effect in 1994.

With the Port of Veracruz poised to benefit from NAFTA, ships will stop at the Mexican Cements Terminal for many years to come.

The treaty has proved a huge boon to the Port of Veracruz. With lower import and export costs, Veracruz has experienced more commercial activity. The trend toward free trade has also pushed Veracruz State to develop better trade relationships with other Mexican and U.S. states along the Gulf of Mexico. In 1995 Veracruz and its Gulf Coast neighbors signed the States of the Gulf of Mexico Initiative, which aims to increase cooperation, tourism, and educational and cultural exchanges among member states. The agreement also includes provisions for the governors of the states to meet each year to talk about free trade. The pact promises to help guarantee that the port of Veracruz will remain a national and world trade leader well into the twenty-first century.

CHAPTER THREE

VERACRUZ AT WORK

Every workday at the Port of Veracruz, thousands of laborers handle more than 4,000 tons of goods, toiling in the heat and humidity of the Gulf Coast climate. Cargo and workers along the docks can seem ant-sized compared to the giant ships in the harbor. The vessels cast shadows that bring the workers welcome escape from the heat of the sun. The ships provide comfort that extends well beyond the waterfront, however. They and the trade items they carry also play an important economic role in the lives of Mexicans, even beyond the state and city of Veracruz.

The Port of Veracruz is like a funnel for incoming and outgoing products. Foreign imports move off ships and into railcars or truck

Trucks await loading at the ICAVE Container Terminal.

43

trailers for the trip to the markets of central and northern Mexico. Likewise goods produced in central or northern Mexican cities come by train or truck to Veracruz to be exported to points all over the world. U.S. citizens provide the biggest foreign market for Mexican products, and U.S. companies supply most of the country's imports. In fact, about three-fifths of Mexico's trade is with the United States. Mexico's other trade partners include the United Kingdom, Germany, Venezuela, Argentina, and Brazil.

A gantry crane carefully lowers a container onto a flatbed truck.

Many facilities at the Port of Veracruz have railway connections that link up with the state of Veracruz's 739 miles of tracks.

Most of the cargoes moving through Veracruz are imports. The top two imports in terms of tonnage are automobile parts and steel plates to be made into cars. In 1996 Veracruz received almost 138 million tons of auto parts and 104 million tons of steel plates. Most of these products come from the United States and travel to Mexico in containers. Trains take the containers, stacked two to a flatbed railcar, to auto manufacturers in cities such as Silao, Puebla, Aguascalientes, and Mexico City in central Mexico, Ramos Arizpe in the north, or Hermosillo far to the northwest.

The majority of imports at Veracruz are bulk cargoes of raw materials. The types of bulk cargoes are broken down into agricultural, mineral, liquid, and general. In 1996 Veracruz's top

At the Grain Terminal, buckets scoop grain from a ship's hold and transfer the cargo to railcars.

agricultural bulk import was corn at 1.7 million tons. The port received 388,400 tons of liquid bulk vegetable oil; 307,800 tons of mineral bulk in the form of scrap metal; and 118,900 tons of general bulk steel cargoes.

Mexican manufacturers turn these raw materials into goods for Mexican and foreign markets. Most of Mexico's highest-value exports are consumer goods traveling in containers. More than 115,700 tons of beer, Veracruz's largest containerized export, traveled through the port in 1996. Appliances are another valuable containerized export. Most major U.S. and Asian appliance companies manufacture goods in Mexico for shipment to North American markets.

➤ In 1996 the breakdown of traffic at the Port of Veracruz was 43 percent agricultural products, 26 percent containerized, 14 percent general cargo, 10 percent liquid bulk, and 7 percent bulk minerals.

Veracruz's agricultural exports include sugar—349,900 tons in 1996—and beans. The port also sent 278,000 tons of liquid bulk molasses and smaller amounts of liquid chemicals to overseas customers. Veracruz shipped out 436,100 tons of steel and concrete tubes for use in construction—the port's largest general bulk export item in 1996. That year the port also handled 119,900 tons of automobiles. Since Mexico has trade pacts with many North American and South American countries, foreign car makers can avoid paying some taxes by assembling automobiles in Mexico. The automobiles travel from their city of manufacture in special truck trailers to the Port of Veracruz, where they are loaded onto ships bound for the United States, Canada, Costa Rica, Venezuela, Colombia, Bolivia, and Chile—all members of the port's vast trade network.

Trucks line up to unload new Mexican-made automobiles for export to consumers in the United States.

BIG THINGS BREWING

What is said to be the best cup of coffee in North America can be found in Veracruz at Café La Parroquia. The coffee is locally grown, but Veracruzans share it worldwide through the vast trade network of which the port is a part.

The coffee comes from the hot and humid highlands of the state of Veracruz. Most of the growers are peasants who own only a few acres of land. Pickers harvest the cherries, or coffee fruits, by hand, and then farmers must cart, carry, or truck their crop to nearby processing plants.

At the plant, the coffee beans, or seeds, are removed from the cherries. The humidity of Veracruz makes it difficult to dry coffee beans the traditional way—in the sun. Instead a pulping machine crushes the beans to loosen their shells. The coffee ferments in tanks of river water until the shells come off.

Laborers then pack the green (unroasted) beans into 60-kilogram (132-pound) burlap bags for the truck ride to the port. Some 52,020 tons of coffee moved through the Port of Veracruz in 1996. Dockworkers load the coffee onto ships for transport to buyers all over the world. Much of the coffee goes to the U.S. port of New Orleans, Louisiana. After the bags arrive at the port of destination, wholesalers or big companies such as Folgers may purchase the coffee. The beans then move onto trucks, trains, or planes bound for warehouses or processing plants, where beans are roasted, ground, and packed into glass or metal containers for sale in supermarkets, restaurants, or coffee shops.

But why do people trade? People and nations exchange what they have for what they want. Trade enables people to eat better foods, to wear different types of clothing, and to live in better homes. Buying and selling within the same country is called domestic trade. Commerce with people or companies in other countries is called international trade.

The buying and selling of goods takes place in a market. Like a grocery store, a market involves customers willing to pay for a product. Items such as coffee, grains, or metals are first traded at a commodity exchange, where people buy and sell contracts for delivery of a product at a certain price on a certain date. The exchange trader then sells the commodity to **wholesalers.** The wholesaler sells smaller quantities to **retailers,** such as grocery stores or supermarkets, for sale to the public. Each time the product is sold, the price increases, and the seller makes a profit. This type of trade is part of a capitalist, or privately controlled, economic system. The idea is that if people decide among themselves what the price of a product should be, then the prices will be fair. Capitalism has proved to be the most successful economic system in history, in terms of personal wealth and higher living standards.

Another type of economic system is communism, in which the government dictates what to manufacture and how to price goods. Often the products are sold for less than what it costs to make them because the government spends its own money to keep prices low for consumers.

A third model, which Mexico follows to a decreasing extent, is a mixed economy. The government makes some of the economic decisions, and private companies and individuals make the rest. A mixed economy gives the people some freedom to choose what is bought and sold while allowing the government to own vital industries such as electricity and to control prices for some commodities. Mexico's economy has become less mixed and more capitalist over the past several years.

No matter what their economic systems, nations do business with one another. Countries often set up trade barriers, or rules and regulations to control how foreign goods are bought and sold. One such barrier is the tariff, a tax paid on a product when it enters a nation. A quota is a limit set by a country on the amount of foreign goods it will accept. Tariffs and quotas can help promote domestic industries that cannot produce things as cheaply as their foreign competitors. Mexico, for example, wanted to build up its domestic auto industry after World War II. For decades Mexican authorities severely limited the number of U.S. cars entering the country. Mexico also placed high tariffs on imported cars. This decision meant that Mexican consumers paid much less for Mexican cars than they did for foreign automobiles. As a result, consumers bought more Mexican cars, a move that helped the industry stay afloat.

But trade barriers can have a backlash effect, too. In addition to the car tariff, Mexico followed an import substitution policy. To replace foreign imports with domestic goods, Mexico set up manufacturing centers in strategic loca-

◀ **Playing by the Rules**

➤ Mexico is the largest supplier of textiles and apparel to the United States. In 1996 Veracruz imported 32,160 tons of cotton for use in the textile industry.

➤ The Port of Veracruz handles about half of all Mexico's container traffic.

50

tions, including Veracruz, to develop the steel, textile, and chemical industries. The government then placed trade barriers on imports of these goods, so that consumers would buy Mexican-made equivalents. But other countries fought back by imposing their own tariffs on Mexican products. Mexican businesses lost sales overseas because their products were suddenly too expensive. With less money coming in from abroad, Mexican consumers didn't have cash to buy goods at home. The result was slower growth for everyone.

Do We Hafta Have NAFTA? Since the 1970s, world markets have been moving toward free trade as a better way to improve domestic industries and to reduce prices on imported goods. Lowering or eliminating trade barriers brings prices down so more consumers can afford things. The policy also forces domestic manufacturers to make their products better and cheaper—or risk going out of business. The more people buy, the more business there is for companies and countries across the globe.

In theory everyone benefits from this kind of trade arrangement. That is why agreements such as NAFTA and the General Agreement on Tariffs and Trade (GATT) are so important to Veracruz and to the rest of the world. GATT spells out the kinds of tariffs that more than 100 countries can levy against one another. Members of GATT, which Mexico joined in 1986, charge lower tariffs to member nations than they do to nonmembers. Veracruz's port authorities estimate that GATT and NAFTA have helped the port's trade grow by about

20 percent since 1992. The States of the Gulf of Mexico Initiative should further reduce the cost of doing business and increase profits for the region.

During the 1990s, the Mexican government de-cided to sell off many state-run industries, including ports. Dozens of companies from inside and outside of Mexico wanted to run port terminals and piers. The Port of Veracruz attracted the most attention. In 1995 ICAVE, which is jointly owned by the Philippine company International Container Services of Manila and by ICA Group of Mexico, bought the right to operate the main container terminal. With that agreement, the Port of Veracruz came full circle—founded by foreigners from Spain, Veracruz is again run largely by outsiders.

 Full Circle

A large part of the port's business happens at the sprawling ICAVE Container Terminal.

Huge tanks at the Fluid Terminals stand ready for a busy day.

The change to private ownership has had a widespread impact on the port. For one thing, Veracruz labor unions agreed to dissolve in exchange for the former union members having first shot at the new jobs. In addition ICAVE has increased its rates for loading and unloading ships to earn back the money spent for upgrading the container facility. Despite the rate hike, the port authority expects that the amount of cargo handled at the port could rise to about 24 million tons by 2002. The boost in traffic will be proof of what a great place Veracruz is to do business—something Mexicans have known for almost 500 years, and something the rest of the world will discover in the next century.

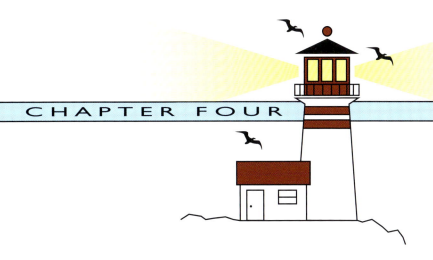

CHAPTER FOUR

GATEWAY TO THE WORLD

A corner of the city of Veracruz juts out into the port. The two will work together to ensure a new century of business.

Just about anywhere one walks in the city of Veracruz, the sights and sounds and smells of the port are ever present. This is especially true in the downtown area, which spreads out from the docks, piers, and warehouses at the water's edge.

Many of Veracruz's most notable features, such as forts, palaces, and protective walls, were constructed to defend or expand the port. About five blocks from the waterfront in downtown Veracruz stands the Baluarte Santiago. The Baluarte, which has been converted to an art museum, is the last remaining section of a large wall built around the city in the early 1600s to protect the area from pirates. San Juan de Ulúa, located on an island in Veracruz harbor, is probably the most imposing and best-known feature in

Vacationers enjoy pedaling a small cart along the malecón, a walkway that follows the waterfront.

Veracruz. The fort was established on the spot where Hernán Cortés and his Spanish troops first landed in Veracruz in 1519. Tourists can wander through the museum, which is a miniature city complete with moats, drawbridges, and walkways.

Veracruz offers plenty of other sights. Right behind the city's main square, Plaza de Armas, which is less than two blocks from the city's beach, a long boardwalk called the *malecón* meanders along the waterfront. Both locals and tourists like to follow the walkway past a local yacht club and numerous shops. From the malecón, visitors can take a boat out to nearby Sacrifices Island to look at ancient ruins or to enjoy the beaches.

➤ Through the centuries, Veracruz was an attractive target for pirates. Lorencillo, a pirate who sacked the city in 1683, was so good at stealing that even today, when Veracruzans can't find something, they say, "Lorencillo took it."

A good place to learn more about Veracruz's history is the City Museum. Constructed in the late 1800s, the building contains artifacts, displays, and models to inform visitors about the city's main features. As one of the cradles of early Mexican civilization, Veracruz is near several significant archaeological treasures. The most notable is El Tajín, an ancient settlement about an hour's drive to the north. Hundreds of buildings remain to be unearthed at El Tajín, but pyramids, ball courts, and homes dot the site.

Closer to the port, the Veracruz Aquarium, the largest in Latin America, is right near the waterfront. The 24-tank aquarium is considered one of the three most important in the world because of its marine research center. Visitors can stand in the middle of a doughnut-shaped tank and watch more than 3,000 kinds of creatures—including sharks, sea turtles, and manta rays—circle around.

There is plenty to see in and around Veracruz. Visitors to the Veracruz Aquarium (above) *peer at turtles, fish, and coral. And the ruins at El Tajín* (right) *provide a glimpse of the region's ancient past.*

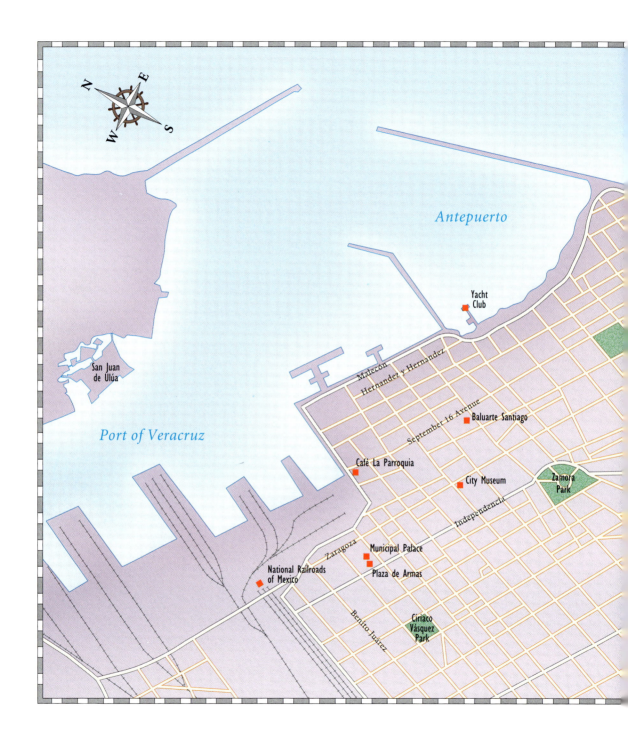

N E
W S

Antepuerto

Yacht
Club

San Juan
de Ulúa

Malecón
Hernández y Hernández

September 16 Avenue   Baluarte Santiago

Port of Veracruz

Café La Parroquia

City Museum

Zamora
Park

Independencia

Zaragoza

Municipal Palace

National Railroads
of Mexico

Plaza de Armas

Benito Juárez

Ciriaco
Vásquez
Park

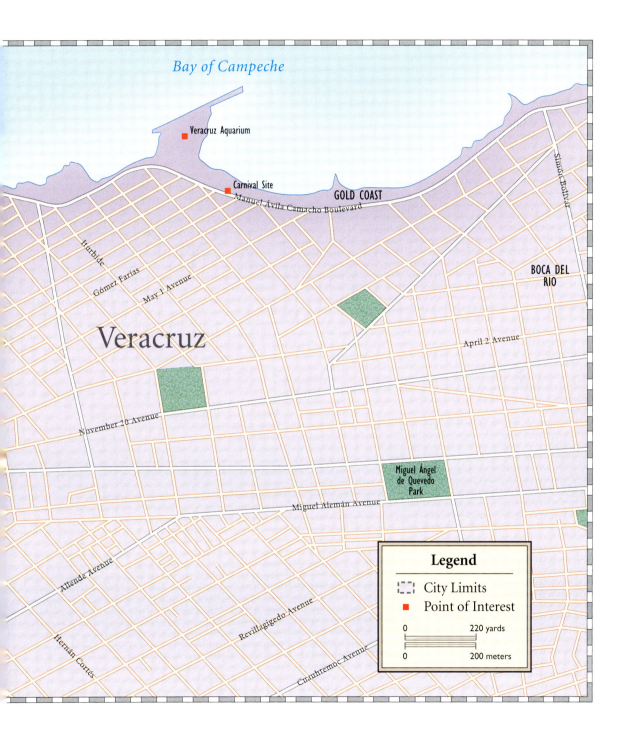

Bay of Campeche

Veracruz Aquarium

Carnival Site

GOLD COAST

Manuel Ávila Camacho Boulevard

Simón Bolívar

Iturbide

Gómez Farías

May 1 Avenue

BOCA DEL RIO

Veracruz

April 2 Avenue

November 20 Avenue

Miguel Ángel de Quevedo Park

Allende Avenue

Miguel Alemán Avenue

Revillagigedo Avenue

Hernán Cortés

Cuauhtemoc Avenue

Legend

⌐ ¬ City Limits
└ ┘

■ Point of Interest

0   220 yards

0   200 meters

59

Since 1994—when APIVER, the port's adminis- ◄ **The Ties That Bind** trative council, was formed—the city and the port have become more connected than ever. Several city officials serve as members of APIVER, the idea being to modernize the city along with the port. The most modern business district in the Veracruz city area is Boca del Río, located a few miles southeast of downtown Veracruz. Until about 1990, Boca del Río was just a sleepy village of only a few thousand people. In the early to middle 1990s, the town was transformed into a modern commercial district with a growth rate almost three times Mexico's national average. The U.S. consulate, which has a business library and the largest Internet center in Mexico, is in Boca del Río. The area also has the best swimming beaches in the Veracruz area. Boca del Río is home to the area's most elegant hotels, which dot a stretch of upscale ocean property called the Gold Coast, and to a World Trade Center, one of only six in Mexico.

➤ The World Trade Center in Boca del Río sponsors talks on everything from cattle to oil exploration, helps local business-people learn about international trade rules, and provides a place where companies can buy and sell their goods.

Veracruz has a well-deserved reputation as the ◄ **The Liveliest City in Mexico** liveliest city in all of Mexico. Although Vera-cruz is not the best-known destination for foreign tourists, the town is especially popular with the people of Mexico City. On weekends Mexico City residents jump into their cars or board the train to make the 240-mile trip to the coast. During Christmas and Easter, it seems impossible to find an empty hotel room in Veracruz. The city is especially animated during the annual Carnival celebration. Carnival is a spirited religious festival in late February or early March. Parades, complete with floats and

60

people in elaborate, colorful costumes, fill the streets during the week-long event, which draws thousands of celebrants. The visitors spend millions of dollars buying everything from food to souvenirs.

Music, dancing, and costumes rule the day at Carnival time.

Even during non-Carnival times, thousands of tourists can be seen walking along the harbor, strolling through downtown, or enjoying the beaches. Every night hundreds of musicians gather at the city's squares and sidewalks to play distinctive Veracruzan marimba music, which features guitar trios and a fast, tropical rhythm. Couples dance the local version of the waltz, called *danzón,* to the marimba music.

A marimba band provides entertainment at a Veracruz night spot.

Even though the music starts playing in the early afternoon, the real action starts when the heat and humidity of the day give way to the cool of the evening. About sunset the activity around Plaza de Armas begins to increase as mariachis (traditional Mexican bands) and marimba groups compete with one another for customers. For a dollar or two per song, the groups play requests or simply serenade listeners. The music goes on until one or two o'clock in the morning. Mixed in with the melodies is the noise of people enjoying themselves in restaurants, bars, and cafes.

Among the musicians and the tourists, hundreds of street vendors sell everything from gum to seashells to stuffed armadillos. The sellers wander about the *zócalo* (town square) and make their way to the tourists lounging or dining at outdoor tables.

➤ Local restaurants serve food prepared *a la veracruzana*—that is, with lots of tomatoes, onions, and chile peppers. Meals often contain seafood, and the best-known dish is red snapper *a la veracruzana.*

Distinctive Character ➤ The arrival of white Spaniards and black Africans dramatically changed the ethnic makeup of the Veracruz area. Over time, as the new arrivals mingled with the locals, the people of Veracruz developed a distinctive character. Spanish became the dominant language, as in all of Mexico. About 85 percent of the city's residents are mestizos, or people with mixed European and Indian ancestry. The addition of African bloodlines has given Veracruzans darker complexions and curlier hair than most Mexicans. Most of the rest of the population are indigenous people who speak native dialects. A very small percentage have only European ancestors.

Veracruz has a rich ethnic heritage that includes people of Spanish, African, and Indian backgrounds.

Growing Pains ➤ Despite its lively attitude, the city of Veracruz faces some problems as it enters the twenty-first century. During the years between 1970 and 1990, the metropolitan area's population nearly doubled, ballooning to about 372,000 by the mid-1990s. The rapid increase placed tremendous pressure on municipal services

63

such as water, electricity, and sewer service. But growth has had its benefits, too. Veracruz has become a city of young people, with an average age of 23. The population is well educated, with a literacy rate of about 94 percent. These people amount to a substantial workforce, which is essential to Veracruz's growing role in international trade.

Veracruz has a very low unemployment rate. Fewer than 5 percent of employable citizens are jobless. The greatest proportion of working Veracruzans have jobs in the service sector. This category includes government, retail, transportation, and teaching.

Blocks and blocks of houses stretch westward from the waterfront.

These port workers are part of Veracruz's service sector. Most of the city's jobs are directly or indirectly connected with the port.

Some 16 percent of Veracruzans work in the manufacturing sector. Only 7 percent of the city's people make their living in construction. And 5 percent work in primary industries such as farming, fishing, and mining—including the oil industry.

In addition to the resident workforce, many foreign businesspeople visit the city of Veracruz on a regular basis. The presence of so many visitors has created a need for everyone from bankers to waiters to know a second language. As a result, the city has experienced a mushrooming of private bilingual schools, in which adults can learn English or French. Most schools tailor their classes to individuals, and the lessons can last anywhere from several months to several years. As a result, English as well as Spanish is sometimes used to do business at the port.

But for all Veracruz's potential, port and city improvements have been hampered by the fact that Mexico is still in the process of developing and modernizing. A high volume of illegal drug trafficking plagues the country, and drug lords sometimes use the beaches of Veracruz State to load and unload their shipments. Mexico also faces widespread government corruption and frequent battles with labor unions over improvements to wages and working conditions. Unions in the state of Veracruz, especially those associated with the oil workers and PEMEX, have often been criticized for their shady dealings. For example, union leaders have been known to take bribes in return for certain decisions or to sell or rent jobs to oil workers. Unions sometimes threaten to strike unless businesses or the government paid them a sum of money. In the late 1980s, however, the president of Mexico jailed the leader of the oil workers' union for corruption. And in 1994, Veracruz port unions disbanded to make it easier for the port to reorganize. The changes have made for a brighter future for the city and port.

As a morning chore, a shopkeeper sweeps his sidewalk. Hard work will keep the shop, the city, and the port running smoothly for a long time to come.

GLOSSARY

breakwater: A seawall that protects a harbor from strong waves and currents.

bulk cargo: Raw products, such as grains and minerals, that are not packaged in separate units. Dry bulk cargo is typically piled loosely in a ship's cargo holds, while liquid bulk cargo is piped into a vessel's storage tanks.

cartel: A small group of nations or companies that join together to control the pricing and distribution of a product.

containerized: Shipped by a method in which a large amount of goods is packed in large standardized containers.

dry dock: A dock where a vessel is kept out of the water so that repairs can be made to the parts that lie below the waterline.

gantry crane: A crane mounted on a platform supported by a framed structure. The crane runs on parallel tracks so it can span or rise above a ship to load and unload heavy cargo.

import substitution: A policy of building up domestic industries so that products made within a country can replace similar imported products.

retailer: A merchant who sells finished products to consumers.

trade winds: Winds that blow constantly in a particular direction. In the past, merchant sailing ships used trade winds to travel between Europe and the Americas, Africa, and Asia.

wholesaler: A merchant who sells products to other merchants, usually retailers, or to manufacturers for further processing.

PRONUNCIATION GUIDE

a la veracruzana	ah lah BEHR-ah-croo-SAH-nah
Antepuerto	AHN-tay-PWAIR-toh
Baluarte	bahl-WAHR-tay
Campeche	kahm-PAY-chay
Cortés, Hernán	kohr-TAYS, air-NAHN
El Tajín	ehl tah-HEEN
malecón	mah-lay-KOHN
San Juan de Ulúa	SAHN HWAHN day oo-LOO-ah
Tenochtitlán	tay-NOHCH-tee-TLAHN
Teotihuacán	TAY-oh-TEE-hwah-KAHN
Veracruz, La Villa Rica de	behr-ah-CROOS, lah BEE-yah REE-cah day
Yucatán	yoo-kah-TAHN

INDEX

METRIC CONVERSION CHART

WHEN YOU KNOW	MULTIPLY BY	TO FIND
inches	2.54	centimeters
feet	0.3048	meters
miles	1.609	kilometers
square feet	0.0929	square meters
square miles	2.59	square kilometers
acres	0.4047	hectares
pounds	0.454	kilograms
tons	0.9072	metric tons
bushels	0.0352	cubic meters
gallons	3.7854	liters

ABOUT THE AUTHOR

Herón Márquez has been a professional journalist since 1979. He has worked as a writer and editor for such newspapers as the *Albuquerque Journal, New York Daily News, Los Angeles Times, Santa Barbara News Press,* and since 1991, the *Minneapolis Star Tribune.* Herón is also the author of Lerner's *Destination San Juan.* He lives in St. Paul, Minnesota, with his wife Traecy.

ACKNOWLEDGMENTS

The book *Lloyd's Ports of the World* (Lloyd's of London Press, 1996) proved invaluable in providing information on the Port of Veracruz. There were also several Internet websites that contained important background on Veracruz and the port. Among them were www.seaportsinfo.com/veracruz.html (the official port website); www.coacade.uv.mx/bruno/ingles/brunoint.html (Bruno Paglia Industrial Park website); www.mexico-travel.com/geninfo/almanac.html#economy (general information on Mexico and Veracruz); and www.mpsnet.com.mx/mexico/veracruz.html (a welcome to the city and state of Veracruz).